HEDGEHOG SURPRISES

HEDGEHOG

SURPRISES

by Betty Jo Stanovich
pictures by Chris L. Demarest

Lothrop, Lee & Shepard Books · New York

For Dad,
with special love
—B.J.S.

To my brother
and sister
—C.L.D.

First Edition 1 2 3 4 5 6 7 8 9 10

Library of Congress Cataloging in Publication Data Stanovich, Betty Jo. Hedgehog surprises.   Summary: Hedgehog and his friend Woodchuck have many adventures including a surprise birthday party with more than one surprise. Sequel to "Hedgehog Adventures."
        [1. Hedgehogs—Fiction.   2. Woodchuck—Fiction]
            I. Demarest, Chris L., ill.   II. Title.
        PZ7.S7932Hg 1984   [E]   83-26820
    ISBN 0-688-02690-7   ISBN 0-688-02691-5 (lib. bdg.)

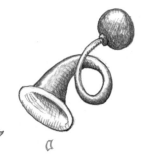

CONTENTS

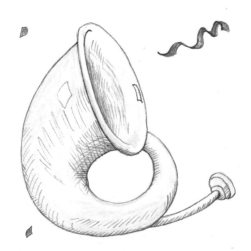

WORRYING

Early one sunny morning
Hedgehog sat on his favorite rock
looking out at the river.

His good friend, Woodchuck,
spied him from the meadow.
"Hedgehog!" he called. "Hello, hello!
Come with me for a walk."

"No!" cried Hedgehog.
"I do not feel like walking."

Woodchuck waded through the tall grass
and climbed down the riverbank.
"Then shall we go visit Old Beaver?"
he asked.

"No, no!" said Hedgehog.
"I do not want to go visiting."

Woodchuck sat on a rock
next to Hedgehog.
"Do you want to eat doughnuts
in the garden," he said,
"now that your flowers are in bloom?"

"No, no, no!" shouted Hedgehog.
"I am too busy to eat doughnuts."

"You do not look busy,"
said Woodchuck.

"I am very busy," said Hedgehog.
"I am busy worrying."

"Again?" said Woodchuck.
"Are you worried about
tonight's party?"

"Oh, no," replied Hedgehog.
"I am worried about
bigger things than that."

"What now?" said Woodchuck.
"Tell me and I shall worry with you.
I am very good at worrying."

"I am worrying about many things,"
said Hedgehog, standing up.
He began pacing back and forth.

"I am worrying," he said,
"that one day
   the rain will stop falling
   and the sun will keep shining,
   and that the river will dry up,
   the plants will dry up,
   everything will dry up—
   even you and me!"
Hedgehog threw up his arms.
He shouted, "What will we do!"

"Hmmm," said Woodchuck.
He stood up too.
He scratched his head,
then he paced back and forth
and around and around.

"Wait!" he cried. "I've got it!
If the rain stops falling,
we will pack our things
and move somewhere else
where it rains as it should.
It may be far,
it may be near,
but we will go together."

"But Woodchuck," said Hedgehog,
"suppose that someday
it rains and it rains.
And then it rains some more!
What if the rain keeps
falling from the sky?

Then the river will surely
flood my house!"
Hedgehog pulled on his spines.
He fell to the ground
and started to sob.

"Wait, I've got it!" Woodchuck shouted,
  shaking his friend.
"If the rain keeps falling,
  you will move in with me!"

"I will?" said Hedgehog, sitting up.

"Yes, of course!" cried Woodchuck.
"Until we can build you
  a brand-new house,
  you can have my spare bedroom."

Hedgehog was quiet for a moment or two.
"Will we have parties?" he asked.

"Oh, yes," said Woodchuck.

Hedgehog smiled a little smile.
Then he asked, "Will we sing songs?"

"Most certainly," replied Woodchuck.

Hedgehog stood up and wiped his eyes.
"And will we have pillow fights
and tell stories in the dark?"

"Every night," said Woodchuck.

"But Woodchuck," said Hedgehog.
"What if you have moved away?"

"I shall never move away,"
  said Woodchuck.

"But you might," said Hedgehog.
"You never know."

"I will only move away,"
  said Woodchuck, "if one day
  the rain stops falling,
  and everything starts to dry up.
  Then we will both move away,
  you and me, together."

Hedgehog followed Woodchuck
up the riverbank.
"You know something?" Hedgehog said.
"You were right, Woodchuck.
You are very good at worrying.
You do it very fast."

"Worrying always goes faster
with two," said Woodchuck
as they raced through the meadow together.

FIZZ

Arising early from his afternoon nap,
Hedgehog studied the plans
for his secret machine.
Then, whirling out of his workroom,
he sang, "How pleased my friends
will be with me
when they see my surprise
for tonight's party."

"Now," he said, "what shall
I make for us to eat?
Black Bear loves poppy seed pancakes.
Since it's his birthday,
I think I will make a batch of those."

So Hedgehog set flour, butter, eggs,
and poppy seeds on his kitchen table.

"But," he said, scratching his head,
"Woodchuck loves cheesy cheesecake.
 Perhaps I should fix that too."

He added milk and cheese
to the table.

"Wait, this won't do!"
 he said with a frown.
"Old Beaver will surely want
 some moon twirl sticks, and Weasel
 some fresh-baked blueberry muffins.
 And the birds always ask for popcorn."

Hedgehog paced back and forth
and around and around.

"I know!" he shouted at last.
"I will make them all.
 What a surprise *that* will be!"

Hedgehog opened every door and
every drawer.
He piled every pot and pan upon
the kitchen table.
Then he measured and mixed,
shaped and stirred,
swirled and twirled,
and patted and poured,
humming his happy song.

He poured the pancake batter into a bowl.
He filled the muffin tins and cake pan.
A cookie sheet of moon twirl sticks
teetered on the chopping board.

"Now," Hedgehog said,
grabbing a big bowl of berries,
"it's time to finish
the biggest surprise of all!"

He sawed and hammered
and nailed and glued,
whistling while he worked.

Hearing the commotion,
Robin, Bluebird, and Sparrow
flew in the window.
Woodchuck, on his way home
from the bakery, peered inside.

"Say, Hedgehog!" called Woodchuck.
"What is that you are making?"

"This is my newest and grandest
   invention," Hedgehog said.
"It is the big surprise
   for my party tonight."

"What does it do?" Woodchuck asked,
   his mouth full of jelly roll.

"Ah," said Hedgehog, smiling
mysteriously. "That is a secret.
When I pull this string," he went on,
"the string will pull the lever,
the lever will turn the funnel,
the funnel will catch something
berry, *berry* special,
which will shoot through this pipe
all the way from here to there,
and birthday surprises will
pop out of my machine!"

Hedgehog pulled the string.
"Ding ding ding," went the machine.

"Why is it dinging?" chirped Robin.

"I don't know," murmured Hedgehog.

"Hmmm," said Woodchuck,
squinting his eyes in thought.
"Maybe it needs some rubber bands
to hold it all together."

"Of course!" cried Hedgehog.
"I am sure that is what it needs!"

Hedgehog stretched dozens of
rubber bands all over his machine.

Then he pulled the string again.

"Ding ding ding, whir whir,"
went the machine.

"Why is it whirring?" chirped Bluebird.

"I'm not sure," said Hedgehog slowly.

"Hmmm," said Woodchuck,
  tilting his head from side to side.
"Perhaps it needs some oil."

"Yes, yes!" Hedgehog exclaimed,
  jumping up and down.
"That is *just* what it needs!"

  Hedgehog oiled his machine.
  Then he pulled the string once more.

"Ding ding ding, whir whir, FIZZ,"
went the machine.

"Why is it fizzing?" chirped Sparrow.

"Why?" shouted Hedgehog. "Why?
Because it is not a great machine.
It is not even a grand machine.
It is a flop, a big fat
fizz machine flop!"
And he huffed off to the kitchen.

Woodchuck pulled another jelly roll
from his bag and munched quietly,
humming a merry tune.

SURPRISES

Hedgehog bustled about his kitchen,
moaning a sad song.
"What will my friends think of me
with no big surprise for my surprise party?"

Suddenly there was a
tap tap tap
upon the front door.

"Oh, no," Hedgehog groaned,
  glancing out the window.
"*Everyone* is early. I had better hurry!"

He scattered poppy seeds here,
and popcorn kernels there.
He stuffed the oven with cheesecake,
moon twirls, and muffins.
Then he rushed off into the next room.

"Greetings!" said Old Beaver.
"We couldn't wait for your party."

"We couldn't wait," said Weasel,
"for a game of croquet."

"Or," growled Black Bear,
"the surprise."

"Of course," said Hedgehog weakly,
  adding, "neither can I."

Hedgehog and his friends
played five games of croquet.
Weasel won all five.

Then they watched the moon,
full and white, rise into the sky.

Something else white rose into the sky.
Hedgehog glanced at his watch,
his spines bristling.
He raced across the lawn,
up the steps, and into the house,
all of his guests in tow.

Hedgehog waded through the smoky kitchen
and threw open the oven door.
A burnt smell filled the air.

"Is this the surprise, Hedgehog?"
called Black Bear through the fog.

"Uh, no," replied Hedgehog.
"This is the signal
that dinner is almost ready.
Poppy seed pancakes, your favorite."

Hedgehog heated four frying pans
and spooned pancake batter into each one.
Soon the room echoed with a sizzling sound.

Suddenly the pancakes started to move.
First a jiggle, then a hop, then a giant leap.

One pancake hit Old Beaver on the nose.
Whap!
Two pancakes buried Bluebird.
And three pancakes landed right on
Black Bear's head.

"Is this your idea of a surprise,
  Hedgehog?" grumbled Black Bear.
"What kind of poppy seeds *are* these anyway?
  They look like popcorn to me."

Hedgehog plopped down on the floor.
He did not know what to say.
His surprises were all flops.

"Black Bear," sighed Woodchuck.
"Don't you know a magic trick
  when you see one?
Popping pancakes are Hedgehog's signal
  that it's time for the surprise."

He handed Black Bear eight plates.
"Now," said Woodchuck, "come along,"
  and he led them all into Hedgehog's workshop.

Five chairs ringed the mysterious machine.
"Sit," said Woodchuck.
Everyone sat except the birds,
who perched atop the berry bowl.
"And now," said Woodchuck,
waving his arms, "the big surprise!
Ready, birds?"

"Ready!" they chirped.

Woodchuck pulled the string on Hedgehog's machine, and the birds ducked their heads into the bowl.

"*Ding ding ding,*" rang the machine.
 Up popped the birds, singing,
"Chirp chirp!"
"*Whir whir,*" rumbled the machine.
"Chirp chirp chirp!" answered the birds.
"*FIZZ,*" finished the machine.
"CHIRP CHIRP CHIRP CHIRP
 CHIRP!" ended the birds.

Woodchuck pulled the string again,
and the concert continued:
ding ding ding
Happy Birthday
whir whir
to you,
FIZZ
Happy Birthday
ding ding ding
to you,
whir whir
Happy Birthday
FIZZ
dear Black Bear,
ding ding ding
Happy Birthday
whir whir
to you
FIZZ.

"What a grand invention, Hedgehog!"
roared Black Bear, clapping.
"And what an unusual surprise party
this has turned out to be.
Thanks to you birds
and thanks to Woodchuck."

"And thanks to Hedgehog," said Woodchuck,
passing the big bag of jelly rolls.

"Well, yes," said Hedgehog,
  filling his plate.
"I knew things would work out
  all right in the end."

"*Ding ding ding,*" went the machine.

Woodchuck winked.

Hedgehog ducked his head
and smiled a big smile.

Betty Jo Stanovich, a native of San Pedro, California, has written two books featuring Hedgehog and Woodchuck as well as *Big Boy, Little Boy,* a picture book illustrated by Virginia Wright-Frierson. A graduate of the University of California at Davis, Ms. Stanovich currently resides in Ann Arbor, Michigan, where she divides her time between writing and teaching.

Chris L. Demarest is the author-illustrator of *Benedict Finds a Home* and *Clemens' Kingdom,* both published by Lothrop. A graduate of the University of Massachusetts, from which he received his B.F.A. in painting, Mr. Demarest lives with his wife, Larkin Upson, in Winchester, Massachusetts.